"Watch out, Pom-pom!"

Oliver had a funny feeling as Irving the skunk raised his tail.

"Watch out, Pom-pom!" Oliver yelled, but the warning came too late.

A terrible stink filled the air. Pom-pom had just been sprayed. The little dog yelped. Then he quickly ran off just as Irving burst out of his cage. The furry skunk ran up the school steps and into the crowded building.

"Yuck! What a stink!" Oliver heard someone yell from inside the school.

"Get me out of here!" someone else cried.

Oliver turned and looked angrily at Stinky Jackson, Irving's owner. But Oliver didn't have time to waste—he had to find Pom-pom, and fast!

OLIVER SMELLS TROUBLE

MICHAEL McBRIER

Illustrated by Blanche Sims

Troll Associates

Library of Congress Cataloging in Publication Data

McBrier, Michael.
    Oliver smells trouble.

    Summary: Anxious to earn some money to buy his
friend Sam a birthday present, Oliver agrees to take
care of a pet skunk.
    [1. Skunks—Fiction.   2. Schools—Fiction]
I. Sims, Blanche, ill.   II. Title.
PZ7.M47828Oo   1988   [Fic]   87-13954
ISBN 0-8167-1149-6 (lib. bdg.)
ISBN 0-8167-1150-X (pbk.)

A TROLL BOOK, published by Troll Associates,
Mahwah, NJ 07430

OLIVER SMELLS TROUBLE

CHAPTER
1

"I'm a worm and I'll squirm on the hook of your lo-o-o-ve!"

Oliver Moffitt rolled his eyes as the sound of the Purple Worms' newest hit came blasting out of Jennifer Hayes's tape recorder. She and her best friend, Kim Williams, bounced in their seats in the school cafeteria. So did Oliver's friend Samantha Lawrence.

"This is the album we're going to play over the PA system on Golliwog Day," said Jennifer. "Isn't it great? It's called the *Purple Worms' Greatest Hits*."

"Yeah, I just *love* the lyrics." Kim added. "They're *so* romantic."

Sam and Oliver laughed.

"Well, I guess anything goes on Golliwog Day," said Oliver.

Sam agreed.

Golliwog Day was the day when everything at school was in reverse. That meant the students ran the school. Sam had been chosen to be principal for the day, and she was determined to make it a Golliwog Day to remember.

"What else are you planning to do, Sam?" asked Oliver.

"Well, of course there won't be any homework that day," she answered. "Plus, I'm going to allow the TV to be turned on in the study room so that the students can watch TV while they do their schoolwork."

"Just like at home," said Kim with a grin.

"And," continued Sam, "I'm going to allow the kids to bring their pets to school!"

"Wow!" exclaimed Oliver. "Now, that's really a *different* idea. It sounds like it's going to be a great day." He often brought pets in to class. But to have *everybody* do it—that would be great!

"Yes, and Jennifer and I are going to have a dance class in the biology classroom," said Kim.

"Why the biology room?" asked Sam.

"Well, can you think of a better place to teach the worm squirm?" answered Jennifer as she turned the volume up. She suddenly started to wiggle up and down in time to the music. A couple of kids nearby giggled and got up to dance. In a little while almost every kid in the cafeteria was wiggling up and down, doing the worm squirm.

Oliver and Sam looked at each other and sighed.

Just then Matthew Farley came over to their table.

"Hi, guys!" cried Matthew as he took out a sandwich and plopped down next to Oliver. "What's up?"

"We're talking about Golliwog Day," said Oliver.

Suddenly Sam sniffed the air.

"What kind of sandwich is *that*?" she asked, wrinkling her nose.

"A spaghetti sandwich!" said Matthew as he took a big bite. "I learned how to make it in my junior gourmet class." Matthew's parents thought that cooking lessons were very important. As well as singing lessons, trumpet lessons, rock-climbing lessons, and karate lessons. Oliver thought his friend spent more time after school in classes than he did in school!

"Spaghetti in a sandwich?" said Kim, who was worm-squirming nearby. "Oh gross! How can you eat that?"

"Like this." Matthew grinned as he sucked up a long strand of spaghetti between his teeth.

"That's *not* what I meant!" said Kim, rolling her eyes.

Matthew looked hurt as he wiped some spaghetti sauce off his chin.

"I need my carbohydrates," he explained. "I have to be in good shape when I give my karate class on Golliwog Day." Matthew chopped at the air with his free hand, almost knocking

Oliver's milk container off the table. "Aaaaaa-aaaaaiiii-yaaaaaaah!" he yelled.

"That should be a lot of kicks!" said Oliver with a grin.

"Ohhh, noo!" groaned Sam. "That has to be the dumbest joke of the day!"

Oliver smiled back at Sam. She was his next-door neighbor and also his best friend.

This year Golliwog Day and Sam's birthday fell on the same day. Oliver wanted to buy her a present. But, as usual, he was short on funds.

He was six weeks overdrawn on his allowance, to buy a new book called *The World's Weirdest Animals*. And it was five weeks since he'd had a customer for his business.

Oliver was the only kid he knew who had his own pet-care service.

Of course, most of the time he took care of dogs and cats when their owners were away. He was also handy with gerbils, fish, and birds.

But he'd also taken care of a camel, an alligator, and a monkey. So he figured, why not broaden his horizons and learn about the care of more exotic animals. And *The World's Weirdest Animals* was just the book he needed.

Suddenly Sam's voice cut into his thoughts.

"Hey, there's Josh!" she said.

The tape had just ended, and all the kids had stopped dancing and had gone back to their seats.

"Josh, come over here!" yelled Sam.

Josh Burns came over, dragging a long sheet of computer paper after him. Everyone knew he was a real whiz at computers. He had been working on a program to use on Golliwog Day.

"What's that, Josh?" asked Oliver.

"It's my new attendance program," answered Josh. "I've just finished running it off on the school's computer. I can't wait to try it out on Golliwog Day."

"Attendance program!" cried Kim. "Josh, how could you be such a . . . a . . ."

"Genius?" answered Josh.

"No—traitor!" said Kim.

Josh looked surprised.

"It's all in the name of science," he said.

"Oh, sure," answered Kim.

But Josh went on as if he hadn't heard.

"I have all the names of the kids in the school entered alphabetically," he explained. "If anyone is absent that day, I simply type his or her name into the computer."

"Then what?" asked Sam.

"Then," answered Josh proudly, "that name automatically gets an 'absent' after it. Not only that, but the computer automatically prints letters to the students telling them that they had better have a good excuse."

"That's fantastic!" cried Sam.

Josh beamed at the group.

"Thanks," he said modestly.

"Yeah, I guess it is okay," joined in Kim.

"Say, Josh, what are you going to do on Golliwog Day?" asked Oliver.

"I thought I would teach a fun science class for the day."

"What's that?" asked Jennifer.

"Oh, just all kinds of tricks, like making an egg fit into a small soda bottle by softening the shell with vinegar and things like that. I'm going to call the class The Magic of Science."

"It looks as if this year's Golliwog Day is going to be the best ever!" Kim grinned.

"You bet!" agreed Oliver. "Just think—trading places with the teachers for one whole day!"

"Well, I don't think it's a fair switch unless we give the *teachers* homework for a change," insisted Jennifer. "To start, Mrs. Muller ought to get at least sixty math problems to do."

Josh grinned. "And I vote that we make Mr. Dillon the gym teacher do two hundred jumping jacks."

"I have an idea! I have an idea!" said Kim. "If any teachers are caught chewing gum, they have to bring a note home to their kids!"

Everyone was giggling wildly, except for Sam. "Come on, you guys," she said. "Do you want this to be the last Golliwog Day, or what?"

"Oh, we'll make it the best ever," Oliver said. "I think we'll have a great time."

"I'll dance to that." Jennifer smiled, turning up her Purple Worms tape again.

By now the whole cafeteria was doing the worm squirm—including Matthew, who just happened to have learned the steps at his dance class the day before.

After school Oliver and Sam went to get their bikes from the bike racks.

"Oliver Moffitt, just the kid I want to see!"
a voice from behind them called.

When they turned around, whom did they
see but Rusty Jackson, heading toward them on
his bike.

"Oh, no," groaned Oliver. "Just the kid I *don't*
want to see!"

"I know what you mean," said Sam. "He's
the biggest bully I know."

"And a real pain in the neck too!" Oliver
added.

As Rusty came closer, Oliver could feel himself tightening up inside.

But surprisingly enough, Rusty was smiling
and waving. Oliver and Sam looked at each
other and raised their eyebrows.

"Why is he being so nice?" asked Sam.

"Maybe he's changed," said Oliver.

"Since yesterday, when he shot spitballs all
over the blackboard?" Sam wondered.

Rusty rode up and gently put on the brakes
just as he reached them. That was a surprise
too. He usually headed straight toward someone as if to knock them down and then screeched
to a stop inches away.

"Hi!" said Rusty, getting off his bike.

"Hi!" answered Oliver and Sam together.

"Um, the reason I wanted to see you, Oliver,"
said Rusty politely, "is that I may have a client
for you."

This was too much! First a gentle Rusty, then
a polite Rusty, and now a Rusty that was giving
him business! Something in the back of Oliver's

head jangled a warning. But he still couldn't see what Rusty could be up to.

Rusty went on.

"I heard that Sam is going to allow pets to be brought into school on Golliwog Day. That reminded me about my cousin."

"Why? Is your cousin a pet?" asked Sam with a little smile.

Rusty laughed good-naturedly.

"Good joke," he said. "But it's just that my cousin is visiting me for a few days and needs someone to watch his pet."

Oliver's interest picked up. Maybe this was his chance to make some money for Sam's present. "What kind of pet is it?" he asked.

"Uh, I'd rather not say," answered Rusty. "I think it would be better if you saw for yourself. All I will say right now is that it's a very *different* kind of pet."

Now Oliver was really interested. This was just what he had wanted, a different kind of pet to take care of.

But Sam took him aside. "I wouldn't trust Rusty if I were you," she whispered. "I just know that he's up to something."

But Oliver needed the money to buy Sam her present. Besides, what could go wrong? If there was one thing he knew about, it was taking care of pets.

"So, whaddaya say?" Rusty looked as if he were getting a little impatient. For a second Oliver thought he sounded just like the old

Rusty. But then Rusty smiled and looked at Oliver questioningly.

"I'll do it," Oliver decided.

"That's great," said Rusty. "I'll meet you back at my house."

With that he hopped on his bike and took off down the street.

When Oliver and Sam arrived at Rusty's house a little while later, they saw Rusty and a smaller kid on the front lawn.

"That must be Rusty's cousin," said Oliver.

Sam nodded.

Rusty motioned them to ride around to the back of the house. When they got there, Rusty and his cousin were waiting for them beside a covered cage. They could hear something sniffing and scratching around underneath the cover.

"Is the pet in there?" asked Oliver.

"Yep," answered Rusty.

Sam looked at the smaller boy.

"Your cousin doesn't talk too much, does he?" she said to Rusty.

Rusty's face took on a sad look.

"He's heartbroken," he said.

Sam was just about to ask why, when Rusty suddenly went over to the cage and whipped off the cover.

"Here's what we want you to take care of," he said. "We're willing to pay good money for it."

Oliver was so surprised at what he saw that he didn't say a word. He just stood there with his mouth open. But Sam took one look and cried, "Oh, no!"

Sam and Oliver went up to the cage to take a closer look at the animal inside. It sniffed at the bottom bars of the cage and looked up with beady bright eyes.

Oliver shook his head and sighed. "Rusty was up to his old tricks after all," he thought.

Because the animal that Rusty wanted him to take care of was a big, furry black-and-white skunk!

CHAPTER
2

"This is Stinky," said Rusty.

"I'll bet," answered Oliver.

"No," said Rusty, pointing to his cousin. "*This* is Stinky. That's Irving in the cage."

"My cousin's staying with us for a few days, and my mom doesn't want Irving in the house," continued Rusty.

"I can imagine," said Sam.

"Yeah," answered Rusty. "That's why Stinky is so sad. He doesn't want Irving to stay out in the cold cruel world all by himself."

Oliver looked at Stinky. He had a sad, innocent look on his face.

"Rusty is telling the truth," Stinky said. "I love that little polecat. Why, I wouldn't be able to sleep at night knowing he was stuck out in the yard in his cage. What if it rained? What if the weather got cold? It's more than I can take.

That's why when Rusty told me about your pet-sitting business, I knew that it was the answer to my prayers."

"Wait a minute," cried Oliver. "What happens when Irving decides to spray something?"

Rusty looked offended.

"Would I give you a skunky skunk?" he answered. "Irving here has been *de-skunked*. He hasn't got one bad smell in his whole furry little body."

"Well, Irving may not smell, but something stinks around here," said Sam. "You're being too nice."

Rusty stared at her for a moment as if he were trying to decide something.

"All right," he suddenly snarled in his old nasty way. "I guess I can't put anything over on you. You're too smart for me."

Oliver and Sam looked at each other. This was the Rusty they knew.

"Look," he said to Oliver. "I'll be honest with you. I didn't want to ask you for favors. But I'm stuck, see? I'm trying to help out my poor little cousin here and you're the only one I know who can take care of Irving."

Sam tugged at Oliver's sleeve.

"We'll have a conference about it," she said as she pulled Oliver aside.

"Be my guest," said Rusty as he held out his hand.

When Sam got Oliver out of Rusty's earshot, she whispered, "I don't trust Rusty. If I were you, I would forget the whole thing."

"But Sam, what could go wrong?" Oliver asked. "Irving is fixed, and now that I think about it, taking care of a skunk would be fun."

"I still say you shouldn't trust him," Sam said. "A skunk is a skunk, Oliver."

"You mean Irving?"

"No, I mean *Rusty!*" said Sam.

"Hey, you guys," yelled Rusty. "Stinky and I haven't got all day. Are you gonna do it or not?"

"Yeah. What's the word?" asked Stinky.

Sam and Oliver walked back to Stinky and Rusty.

"You have a deal," said Oliver.

"That's more like it," said Rusty.

"But I'll have to ask you to pay in advance," said Oliver, thinking about Sam's present.

Rusty looked at his cousin and then back at Oliver.

"No problem," answered Rusty with a grin.

"But don't forget," said Stinky. "I want visitation rights! I just know that Irving will miss me, and I would like to be able to come over whenever I want to."

"I guess that would be okay," answered Oliver. "But please call first. My mom doesn't like surprise visits."

It was already dark when Oliver and Sam turned into the Moffitts' driveway. Oliver had Irving's cage tied securely to the rack at the back of his bike. Sam still didn't agree with

21

Oliver's decision to take care of Irving. But she was too good a friend not to help him now that he had made the choice.

As they pulled up to Oliver's front door, they could hear Pom-pom barking. Pom-pom was Mrs. Moffitt's dog. He was a Shih Tzu from China. But even though he was small, Pom-pom could be very pushy when he wanted to be.

"It sounds like Pom-pom wants to go out for his walk," said Sam.

"Yeah," agreed Oliver. "As soon as I bring Irving in, I'll take Pom-pom out."

"I'll give you a hand," said Sam.

"Thanks," answered Oliver as he got off his bike.

Sam went over to the back of Oliver's bike. She bent down and lifted the cover of Irving's cage. Instantly Irving came up to her face and twitched his little nose. Sam jumped back in surprise. Then Irving lifted his head and sniffed the air.

"Don't worry," said Oliver softly. "You're going to be happy here. Just wait until you meet Pom-pom. He's the friendliest little dog you've ever seen."

"Oh, Oliver!" cried Sam. "Stop talking to that skunk as if he understands you."

Oliver smiled. "Animals don't have to understand the words," he said. "It's the *way* you say them."

Oliver stepped up to the front door. Just as he put the key in the lock, he spotted a note. "Oliver," it said in his mother's handwriting. Trust

Mom to keep things organized. She and Oliver ran the house—Oliver hadn't seen his father since he was a baby.

Unfolding the note, Oliver read:

Please use the kitchen door and keep out of the living room. I'll be home at 6:00.
Love,
Mom

Oliver remembered that his mother had planned to wax the living-room floor that morning. And he knew how his mother was about freshly polished floors. He'd be lucky if he'd get in there at all today!

Stuffing the note into his pocket, Oliver walked around to the side of the house and entered the kitchen.

"Yip! Yip! Yip!" There was Pom-pom, looking a little restless and dazed.

"I guess you weren't allowed in the living room either, huh, boy?" laughed Oliver. "Well, I have something that will cheer you up."

Pom-pom wagged his tail, panting excitedly.

"Okay, Sam," Oliver called out the kitchen

window. "You can bring Irving in now." But as he turned away from the window, Oliver realized he'd forgotten to tell Sam to use the side door.

Quickly he pulled aside the gate that blocked off the living room, "Hey, Sam, I was going to tell you . . ."

But Sam had already opened the door. She stood on the polished living-room floor, which glistened like an ice-skating rink. "Where do you want me to put this?" she asked, holding Irving's cage in front of her.

Just then Pom-pom let out a high, screeching yelp. He had spotted the skunk in the cage. Darting around Sam, he jumped up, trying to get at Irving.

Irving squeaked and spun around. He wanted to get at Pom-pom.

"Hey, what's . . ." said Sam, lifting the cage. She stepped back and began to slip. "Whooo-oooah!" she yelled, falling back with a bump.

"Sam! The cage!" shouted Oliver.

But there wasn't much that Sam could do. Irving's cage was out of her hands. It flew across the room and landed with a crash. The door of the cage popped open. Poor Irving tumbled out.

Sam and Oliver tried to run to the skunk. But they slipped on the polished floor. Pom-pom slid too, then got his footing, and bounded across the room. Irving took one look and started to climb a potted rubber plant.

"Oh, no!" cried Oliver. "Not the plant!"

Too late. The pot tipped over, spilling Irving,

the plant, and wet, sticky soil all over the shiny floor!

Both Pom-pom and Irving skittered through the dirt, leaving two muddy paths of footprints. But just as Oliver charged up, trying to grab them, both animals leaped onto the sofa.

"Oh, no!" Oliver moaned. "Not the new white sofa!"

But it was too late again. Two lines of dirty paw prints now decorated the cushions on the sofa.

Next to the once-white sofa, on a mahogany table, was a big, expensive vase. It had been given to Oliver's great-grandmother when she worked as a chef for a wealthy old woman. Now Pom-pom and Irving were chasing each other around and around the vase. Suddenly Irving leaped up to the rim and disappeared inside. The vase began to topple back and forth!

"Oh, no!" screamed Oliver. "Not Lady Swansong's vase! Anything but Lady Swansong's vase!"

Sam held her breath and covered her eyes.

"Do something!" Oliver thought to himself. The vase was about to tip over.

Oliver imagined sliding to first base. "Ah-ha!" he said out loud. Then with all his might he jumped and slid across the slippery floor, his arms stretched out in front of him. Sam cheered wildly as Oliver reached the table just in time to catch the priceless vase.

"Safe!"called Sam, spreading her arms.

"Not quite," said Oliver.

Standing in the doorway just behind Sam was a horrified Mrs. Moffitt. She held her hands up to her head and looked at the mess in the room. "What on earth is going on around here?" she asked.

"Oh, I can explain, Mom," Oliver said.

But that was the moment Irving chose to poke his muddy head out from inside the vase. He squeaked and wiggled his little nose as he looked at Oliver's mother.

Mrs. Moffitt jumped back. "Oliver," she said. "Is that what I think it is?"

"Uh-oh," whispered Sam to Oliver. "I think I smell big trouble."

CHAPTER
3

The next morning at breakfast, Oliver paid a lot of attention to his pancakes, even though he wasn't really hungry. He poured syrup carefully over the stack and watched it drip down the sides. He stared as little rivers formed on the plate.

Out of the corner of his eye he saw his mother sitting at the table.

"I think we should have a little talk now," Mrs. Moffitt finally said.

Oliver nodded. After cleaning things up last night, his mother had been too upset to talk. She had just told Oliver to take the skunk out to the garage and that they would talk about things in the morning.

"I wish you had asked me before bringing a skunk into our house," she said.

"But Mom, I told you, Irving's de-skunked. There's no way he can smell up the house."

"That may be true," his mother answered. "But there are other things to consider. He and Pom-pom are not going to be the best of friends."

Oliver had to admit that his mother was right. Even now Pom-pom was at the kitchen door, whining and scratching. The little Shih Tzu knew that Irving was in the garage, and he looked as if he couldn't wait to have another shot at the skunk.

Oliver looked up at his mother. Suddenly she smiled and said, "I know that the whole thing was an accident. I guess you didn't know that dogs and skunks don't get along."

"I sure do now," Oliver sighed.

"Then you understand why that skunk has to go," said Mrs. Moffitt.

"Please let me take care of Irving, Mom," Oliver begged. "I promise that he'll be no trouble from now on. Besides, I need the money to buy Sam a present for her birthday."

Mrs. Moffitt smiled again. "Why, that's very thoughtful of you," she said. Then she went back to the stove and fiddled with the frying pan. Her brow was furrowed. Oliver knew what that look meant. It meant that she was trying to decide about something.

"Okay," she finally said. "You can take care of Irving if you promise to do two things."

"Name them!" said Oliver.

"Keep Irving in the garage and keep Pom-pom away from him," she answered.

Oliver jumped up from his chair and gave his mother a hug.

"Thanks, Mom—you can count on me!" he cried.

"Oh, and there's a third thing," said his mother.

"What's that?" asked Oliver.

"Finish your breakfast," she answered.

Oliver smiled and sat down again. He picked up a big forkful of pancakes and put it in his mouth. Suddenly he felt very hungry.

That afternoon Oliver was hauling branches and stones into the garage. He had gathered them from around the yard. He was glad that it was Saturday and there was no school. He could spend all day making sure that Irving was comfortable. He had found a chapter on skunks in *The World's Weirdest Animals*. It said that skunks liked to stay in their dens during the day and come out at night to hunt. So he had to figure out a way of giving Irving a den.

Just then Sam came in. Jennifer, Josh, Kim, and Matthew trailed after her.

"Hey, Oliver," called Matthew as they came into the garage. "Sam told us about your skunk. Can we see him?"

Oliver pointed to a dark corner of the garage, where he had put Irving.

"Sure," he said. "He's over here. But be careful, I don't want him to get excited."

Everyone followed Oliver to where Irving was.

"Oh, gross," said Jennifer as she peered into the cage.

"Coming from someone who likes purple worms, that's funny," Oliver replied.

Everyone laughed and Jennifer turned red.

"Well, I still think skunks are gross!" she said. "And Kim does too. Don't you, Kim?"

Kim looked surprised and said, "I do?"

Everyone laughed again. Kim shrugged and took a long look at Irving. "I don't know," she said. "I think he's kind of cute."

Matthew and Josh were fascinated too.

"What are you going to do with all those branches and stones?" asked Matthew.

"I'm going to build Irving a little den in the corner of the garage," answered Oliver. "That way he'll feel at home during the day."

"What about at night?" asked Sam.

"I guess I'll have to keep him in his cage at night," answered Oliver. "I'll just make sure that he has enough to eat."

"What do skunks eat?" asked Josh.

"Oh, insects, eggs, lizards—things like that," said Oliver with a smile.

"Oh, *double* gross!" cried Jennifer. "Imagine eating insects."

"But they'll also eat things like apples and oranges and grain," he added.

"And what about his scent glands?" Josh gave Irving a very careful look. "Aren't you afraid he's going to stink up the whole garage if he gets mad or frightened?"

"Oh, no," said Oliver. "Irving's been de-skunked."

"How are skunks de-skunked?" asked Kim.

"Their scent glands are removed when they're young," said a voice from the front of the garage.

Oliver turned around to see Stinky Jackson walk in.

"I just came over to see how my little polecat is doing," explained Stinky. He walked up to the cage and looked in. Irving had been huddled in a corner. But when he saw Stinky, he got up and scurried over. As he reached Stinky, the little skunk raised his head and twitched his nose.

"Hello yourself," said Stinky.

Then he turned to face everyone and said, "As I was saying, they remove a skunk's scent glands when it's still young. After that they make great pets."

"And it's a good thing too," said Sam. "I heard that a skunk's spray can make you stop breathing!"

"Only for a few seconds or so," answered Stinky. "But that's enough to frighten off any animal, after it gets a whiff!"

"I heard that a skunk's spray can be smelled from a mile away," said Josh.

"That's true," answered Stinky, "if the wind happens to be blowing in the right direction."

"Not only that," Oliver cut in, "but if you ever get any spray on your clothes, you would have to wash them a million times to get the stink out."

"Also true." Stinky smiled.

"Wait a minute," said Matthew. "I read somewhere that you can take out a skunk's smell with tomato juice."

"That's right," answered Oliver. "But who wants to go around smelling like a ripe tomato?"

Stinky laughed. "Hey, why are we talking about smelly skunks anyway? Irving smells as sweet as a flower. He's as good a pet as a dog or a cat."

"I only wish I were going to your school," he went on. "I would have loved to bring in Irving on Golliwog Day!"

Oliver snapped his fingers.

"Hey, that's a great idea," he said. "Why don't I take Irving to school on Golliwog Day?"

"That *is* a great idea," said Kim.

Then Oliver realized that he hadn't asked Stinky's permission. He turned to Rusty's cousin and said, "That is, if it's all right with you."

Stinky looked as if he were thinking it over. Then he shrugged and said, "Why not? As long as you can promise me that he'll be carefully watched."

"Of course," answered Oliver.

"Then it's settled," said Stinky.

Oliver felt great. He was learning how to take care of a skunk, and he was making money too.

Oliver knew exactly what he was going to get Sam for her birthday—a bottle of Spring Water perfume. She had told him just the other day that she loved the scent of it.

Stinky interrupted his thoughts. "Well, I can see that you are doing a good job with Irving," he said. "So I'll run along now and play ball with my cousin."

"A nice kid," Oliver thought as Stinky walked away.

"It's hard to believe that he's related to a zero like Rusty Jackson!" said Matthew.

CHAPTER
4

Oliver and Sam walked into the Moffitts' kitchen carrying a flat white box. The delicious smell of pizza filled the room. "This was a good idea," Sam said. "I feel as though I haven't seen you for a week!" She bent over to sniff the mouth-watering pizza smell again.

That made Oliver think of another scent—the perfume he'd bought for Sam's birthday. He had just bought the bottle that day. It was all wrapped up, tied with a red ribbon, and hidden in his closet. He couldn't wait to give it to her tomorrow.

"It's just been two days," Oliver said. "You were busy and so was I. Now everything is all set with Irving."

Oliver opened the box and nearly tripped as Pom-pom circled his feet, whining. Pizza was Pom-pom's favorite food.

"I can't believe tomorrow is Golliwog Day. I still have so much to do," said Sam.

"Like what?" asked Oliver.

"Well, for one thing, I need a few more monitors for the hallways," answered Sam. "I've already asked Matthew and he said yes. And I'm going to ask Harvey Woodman."

"That sounds good," said Oliver. "If anybody gets out of line, Matthew can karate-chop them."

"But I still need one more monitor," Sam went on.

"Hey, how about Rusty Jackson?" suggested Oliver.

"Rusty Jackson!" said Sam. "He's the last one I would ask. Why, most of the time he needs someone to monitor *him*!"

"I don't know," said Oliver. "Rusty's been very good these past few days. In fact, just yesterday he told me that he wished he could do something to help out on Golliwog Day."

Sam looked doubtful.

"You think about it while I get some plates and things for our pizza," said Oliver.

Oliver's mother was coming home late that night, and she had given Oliver some money to buy supper for himself and Sam. The two friends had just come from the Pizza Palace on Sutherland Avenue, where they had picked up a deluxe pizza.

"Maybe you're right," Sam said to Oliver. "Being a monitor might keep Rusty out of trouble."

"See? One problem down," said Oliver with a grin. "Anything else?"

"Just a few telephone calls that I'll make later at home," said Sam, eyeing the pizza hungrily.

"Great! Now, let's eat!" Oliver sat down, rubbing his hands.

The minute they lifted the lid of the box, Pom-pom practically jumped on the table. Oliver groaned. "Give me a break, Pom-pom! You know you're not supposed to eat human food!"

"Oh, Oliver! Pizza isn't just human food," sighed Sam, taking a big whiff of the steaming pie. "It's the food of the gods!"

Oliver shrugged and tore off a tiny piece of pie. He tossed it to Pom-pom, who made it disappear in one gulp.

Sam was about to toss him another scrap when Oliver stopped her.

"That's enough. I promised Mom I wouldn't let Pom-pom or Irving get out of hand anymore. She's still recovering from the 'great living-room disaster.' "

Pom-pom started to whine. He dragged himself to the corner of the kitchen, his eyes never leaving the pizza.

"Oh, all right," said Oliver.

Sam tossed him a tiny piece. Pom-pom caught it on the fly and gulped it down. But a little slower this time.

"Now, that's all," said Oliver sternly. "If it were up to him, he'd eat the whole pizza—*and* drink up all our root beer."

Sam laughed and picked up her slice. Oliver

and Sam were happy to be spending time together. Sam hadn't seen Oliver since she was so busy with preparations for Golliwog Day. "How's Irving?" she asked, while chomping on pizza crust.

"Great," answered Oliver. "He seems to love the den I made for him. He stays in it a lot during the day. Of course, I have to make sure the garage door is closed so he doesn't wander off."

"Does Stinky come over to visit him?" asked Sam.

"He comes once in a while," answered Oliver. "Boy, it was really nice of Rusty to tell Stinky about my pet-care business."

"Yeah," said Sam, twisting a piece of stringy cheese off her next slice. "Maybe Stinky is a good example for him."

They were down to the last slice of pizza when Oliver remembered that he'd promised his mother to save her some.

"That's okay with me," said Sam. She stood up from the table, patting her stomach. "I think I'm pepperonied-out!"

They cleaned up the kitchen. Then Sam said she had to leave.

"I'll see you first thing in the morning," she called as she went out the door.

Oliver waved good-bye.

"I think I'll go into the garage and take care of Irving," he said. "It's time to put him in his cage for the night."

When Pom-pom heard "Irving," he barked

loudly and ran to the kitchen door. That was a word that he had learned to recognize very quickly. He sniffed and scraped at the bottom of the door, wagging his tail.

"Forget it, Pom-pom," said Oliver. "There's no way I'm going to let you and Irving get together again."

He shooed Pom-pom away from the door and quickly left.

When he got to the garage, he saw Irving slowly moving around the outside of his den.

"Hi, Irving," he said. "I'm sorry, but I have to put you away for the night. We can't have you running around the neighborhood hunting for food."

Irving moved away from his den and came to Oliver, lifting his head and twitching his nose. Oliver picked him up and put him into his cage. Then he made sure that Irving had enough carrots and apples to last him the night. He was just about finished when he heard his mother calling from the house.

"Oliver, I'm home," she called. "Are you in the garage?"

"Yes, Mom," Oliver shouted back. "I'll be right in."

Oliver ran to meet his mother at the front door.

"What a day!" sighed Mrs. Moffitt. As soon as she opened the door and entered the house, Oliver's mother headed straight for the sofa— which now wore a flowered slipcover. She wasn't going to take any more chances with her new white sofa.

Oliver went to the kitchen to get his mother's dinner. But when he got to the table, he stopped cold in his tracks. The pizza box was turned over on the floor. And right beside it was Pom-pom! He was devouring the last slice!

"So this is why you didn't come to say hello to Mom!" Oliver frantically wiped the tomato sauce and cheese off the little dog's face. How could this happen after he'd promised his mother there wouldn't be any more trouble?

Oliver heard his mother calling from the living room. "My mouth's been watering for pizza all day," Mrs. Moffitt said. "How about my slice?"

Oliver froze. "Oh, too bad, Mom," he called back. "Sam and I didn't have pizza for dinner . . . um . . . they were all out."

"Pizza Palace was all out of pizza?" cried Mrs. Moffitt.

Oliver winced. He was never good at coming up with excuses.

"Oh, well," he heard his mother say. "I suppose a cup of hot chocolate and cookies would be nice."

"Terrific!" said Oliver. "I—I mean . . . terrific choice, Mom." He made a face at Pom-pom as he prepared his mother's snack.

Oliver came back to the living room with a steaming cup in one hand and a plate of cookies in the other. His mother took the cup of hot chocolate and sipped at it carefully.

"Mmmmmm, good," she murmured. "You

have got to be the best hot-chocolate-maker in town."

"Aw, shucks," Oliver smiled in pleasure. He was happy and relieved that his mother had forgotten about the pizza. Now, if she just didn't smell the pepperoni on Pom-pom's breath . . .

After she had finished the hot chocolate and eaten some of the cookies, Mrs. Moffitt said, "I'm going to have to get up extra early tomorrow. We're working on an important project in the office."

"That's okay, Mom," said Oliver. "I can get my own breakfast. And I'll make sure Pom-pom is okay before I leave."

Suddenly Mrs. Moffitt tapped her forehead with her fingertips.

"Omigosh! I almost forgot," she cried. "Pompom has an appointment at the vet's tomorrow. He has to get a checkup and his yearly shots! And I won't be able to take him in the car."

Oliver was silent for a moment, then he said, "I've got an idea. The vet's office is near the school anyway. I can take Pom-pom in my bike basket and drop him off for you."

"That would help a lot," said his mother.

Oliver was all set to congratulate himself, when he suddenly tapped his forehead just as his mother had done. "Oh, no!" he cried.

"What's wrong?" asked his mother.

"I almost forgot too!" he answered. "Tomorrow is Golliwog Day and I'm supposed to bring Irving into school. I sure can't put him and

Pom-pom in the same basket. There'll be a dog-polecat war!"

His mother looked at him.

"I think we have a problem," she said.

Suddenly Oliver snapped his fingers.

"Wait a minute," he cried. "I'll ask Sam to help me! Maybe she can take Irving on *her* bike!"

He quickly got on the phone and called Sam.

"Gosh, Oliver," she said after he explained his problem. "I would love to help you, but I can't. I have a load of stuff to bring to school. And I'm not sure I can fit all of that on my bike."

After Oliver finished talking to Sam, he tried dialing Matthew.

"Sorry, Oliver," sighed Matthew. "But I have my junior gourmet class tomorrow."

"Before school?" Oliver burst out.

"We're cooking breakfast," explained Matthew.

"Oh." Oliver hung up the phone, feeling very glum.

"I guess it's not going to work, is it?" said his mother. "You look as if you don't know whether you're coming or going."

Coming or going!

That saying gave Oliver an idea. He grinned. "No problem, Mom."

"No problem?" Mrs. Moffitt echoed.

"I can put Irving in his cage and tie that to the *back* of my bike on the rack. Then I can put Pom-pom in the basket in *front*! They'll be separated, and I'll be in the middle. There's no way that they can get at each other."

His mother nodded.

"Well, it sounds as if it might work, but are you sure you can handle both of them?"

"Sure," answered Oliver. "I'll just drop off Irving at school and give him to Sam. Then I'll take Pom-pom to the vet's and be back at school in plenty of time for Golliwog Day!"

He ran to the phone in the kitchen and quickly dialed Sam's number again. When Sam answered the phone, he told her his idea. Sam agreed it was a good one. She told Oliver that she'd be glad to watch Irving for him at school.

"I guess I'm getting used to the little stinker myself," she said with a chuckle.

Oliver sighed with relief. He was about to join his mother in the living room, when he saw the pizza box. If his mother saw it, she'd know for sure they'd had pizza—and then she'd find out about Pom-pom!

Quickly he bundled up the box and headed out the kitchen door.

"Where are you going, Oliver?" asked Mrs. Moffitt when she heard the door opening.

"Just taking out the garbage, Mom!"

"Really?" said Mrs. Moffitt. "Usually I have to do a headstand on a pyramid to get you to do that."

Oliver scurried out.

While he stood in the chilly night air, stuffing the crumpled pizza box into the giant trash can, he stopped short. He could have sworn he heard the garage door close.

Oliver walked slowly toward the front of the garage. He strained his ears, and heard the sound of rustling leaves—as though someone were running away. But as he peered into the darkness, Oliver could see no one.

He crept up to the garage door and swung it up. Everything inside looked just the way it always did. Even Irving was sitting quietly in his cage. Oliver shook his head. It couldn't have been Stinky. Stinky always politely called Oliver before he dropped by to visit Irving.

Then what was that noise?

"Oh, well," thought Oliver a bit nervously. "Time to go inside." With a shiver he shut the garage door and headed back to the house.

CHAPTER 5

Oliver woke up extra early. He jumped out of bed and looked out the window. The sun was shining, the sky was blue, and the weather was mild. It was going to be perfect weather for Golliwog Day! Oliver practically forgot about the weird noises he had heard the night before.

He hurried into the kitchen. His mother was just about to leave for work.

"Good morning, Oliver," she said. "I was just putting out your orange juice and cereal."

"Thanks, Mom," said Oliver.

Then his mother looked at the time.

"Well, I'd better go. I don't want to be late for work, especially today."

"I have Pom-pom all ready for his trip," she continued. "He's already eaten and I've taken

49

him out for a short walk. Are you sure that you're going to be all right?"

"No problem, Mom," Oliver answered. "I'll be fine."

His mother bent down and gave Oliver a kiss.

"Well, have a great time at school," she said. "I should be home at my regular time tonight."

" 'Bye, Mom," replied Oliver.

As soon as Oliver finished breakfast, he got dressed. Then he took his knapsack and put Sam's present in it. After he checked that everything in the house was in order, he went to the garage.

The first thing he did when he got there was go to Irving's cage. Irving looked up and sniffed the air.

"Morning, Irving," said Oliver. "I'm afraid you're going to have to stay in your cage a little while longer today."

He took the cage and loaded it onto the rack at the back of his bike. He made sure it was tied securely in place.

"There, now you're all ready for your trip to school," he murmured. "I just have one more thing to do and we can all leave."

He took a flat piece of cardboard and punched some holes in it. Then he tied the cardboard to the top of his bike basket. He wanted to make sure that Pom-pom wouldn't jump out of the basket along the way.

Just then he could hear Pom-pom barking from inside the house. "He must know I have

Irving out," thought Oliver. But he didn't worry too much about Pom-pom. After all, his plan was foolproof, wasn't it?

He brought his bike to the front of the house, opened the door, and grabbed the little Shih Tzu. Pom-pom began licking his face. But when he saw Irving on the back of the bicycle, he growled and tried to wiggle out of Oliver's arms.

"Take it easy, Pom-pom!" Oliver said sternly. "You'll just have to grin and bear it until we get to school—if dogs can grin, that is."

He put Pom-pom into the bike basket and tied down the cardboard lid. Then he quickly hopped on the bike, pedaling his way toward Sutherland Avenue. With Oliver in the way, Pom-pom couldn't see Irving. Soon he quieted down.

"There, now," said Oliver to Pom-pom cheerfully. "This isn't so bad, is it?"

Pom-pom let out a soft bark. He really seemed to be enjoying the ride. There was a light breeze, and the dog loved it when the wind blew in his face.

Everything was going along perfectly as Oliver reached Sutherland Avenue. Although it was early, the street was already full of people. And since the weather was warm, a lot of store owners had displays in front of their stores.

Webley's Department Store had a rack full of what looked like fur coats on display. On the window of the store a sign read: FABULOUS FAKES ON SALE! FAKE OUT THE WINTER CHILL!

From his bicycle Oliver could see that the coats looked like wild jungle animals. That was appropriate, considering the way the shoppers were clawing at them.

As Oliver pedaled along the bike path, the wind suddenly changed direction. Now it blew from behind him. Pom-pom sniffed the air. Then he began to bark and growl, scratching at the side of the basket.

"Oh, no," thought Oliver, "he's picking up Irving's scent!" Pom-pom was also jumping up and hitting the cardboard cover. Any minute now it could come off!

Oliver was so distracted by Pom-pom that he jumped the curb and found himself on the sidewalk. It was then that Pom-pom broke the cover and tried to leap out of the basket.

"Get down, Pom-pom!" yelled Oliver.

He tried to hold the cover down with one hand and steer with the other. The bike zig-zagged down the sidewalk, heading straight for the fur coat display!

"Hey! Watch where you're going!" yelled a woman whom he had just missed hitting.

"Crazy kid!" said someone else.

"Mark my words, Ethel," said an elderly man to his wife. "First it's bicycles, then it's motor-cycles!"

But Oliver didn't have time to pay attention to what people were saying. He had his hands full with his bike. It was wobbling wildly now, and Pom-pom was busily trying to wiggle out from under his hand.

Suddenly Pom-pom jumped free and landed on the sidewalk. "Come back, Pom-pom!" Oliver yelled. Then he turned around quickly.

But he needn't have bothered. Pom-pom wasn't running in the other direction. He was chasing Oliver down the street, still trying to get at Irving. In the meantime, Irving was being tossed around in his cage by the bumpy ride.

Staring back at the little dog, Oliver was just about to put on his brakes and scoop him up. Then someone yelled, "Look out!"

Oliver turned to face forward and saw that he was headed straight for the fur coat rack!

"Oh, noooo!" Oliver yelled. Unable to stop his bike, he rolled right through the coat rack. Oliver came out the other side with a huge, furry tiger-skin coat draped over his head and body.

"Hey! I was going to buy that coat!" screamed an angry shopper. "I saw it first!"

All of a sudden, Mr. Quincy, the manager of Webley's, came running out of the store. He took one look at Oliver whizzing down Sutherland Avenue in the Pepe of Paris original and began jumping up and down, shaking his fists. "Stop, thief!" he yelled as the carnation on his jacket began to wilt.

Oliver tried to stop. But he couldn't find his handlebar brake under the heavy tent of a coat.

Just around the corner a policeman was giving a ticket to an illegally parked car. A little

boy ran over to him excitedly. "Hey, Mister Policeman! There's a great big tiger riding a bicycle down Sutherland Avenue."

The policeman threw back his head and laughed. "A tiger? Now, sonny, we all know that tigers don't ride bicycles!"

At that very moment Oliver skidded around the corner and zigzagged right past the policeman.

"Hey, you! Ti-ti-tiger! Stop!!" he shouted. The officer ran in front of Oliver's bike and held out his arms. Oliver was still desperately trying to brake, when he crashed right into the policeman!

They all fell down in a tangled heap—Oliver, the bike, the fur coat, and the officer. But since the bike fell on top of the coat, Irving wasn't hurt. Poor Irving was just shaken up. And Pom-pom was nowhere to be seen.

"Officer, I can explain everything...." Oliver began.

"Oh sure," said the policeman, "I've heard that one before."

But when Oliver explained what had happened, the officer did believe him. In fact, he even offered to help find Pom-pom—after they had returned the fake fur coat.

Nat, the owner of the pretzel cart, told them that he'd seen a little dog running into Webley's Department Store.

They raced to the store and started searching, but Pom-pom was nowhere to be found. As they passed the hat counter, a woman in a fur coat was saying, "I want something to match my coat. Something like . . . this one!"

She reached out toward a black-and-white ball of fur, but then she jumped back, screaming.

"Madam, what is the problem?" asked the manager.

"Th-tha-that hat just growled at me!" stammered the woman.

Oliver's face lit up with a smile. "Pom-pom!" he cried. "How did you ever get there?" He walked over to the counter and lifted the frightened little dog off the shiny glass case.

"Thanks for helping me find my dog, Officer!" Oliver said to the policeman.

As Oliver and Pom-pom left the store, Mr. Quincy rolled his eyes. He sighed at the smiling policeman. "And it isn't even the holiday rush!"

Outside again, Oliver put Pom-pom into the basket and closed the lid. The little dog seemed to have gotten tired of growling and whining, and now lay down quietly in his basket. Even Irving seemed exhausted by all the excitement. He had curled himself up in a corner of the cage and looked as if he were napping.

But Oliver didn't want to take any more chances. He decided to walk his bike the rest of the way to school. He had only six blocks to go.

When Oliver got to the school, he saw Sam, Rusty, and Stinky waiting at the entrance.

Sam ran up to him.

"What happened to you?" she asked. "I was worried. You should have been here half an hour ago."

"Yeah," said Rusty. "So were we. We thought maybe something happened to Irving."

Oliver took the cage off the back of his bike and put it on the ground a short distance away.

"Irving's fine, as you can see," he said.

Then he told them what had happened.

"Gosh," said Stinky. "We're sure glad that you're okay now."

"Thanks," said Oliver. "I was a little worried when I fell. I was sure I was going to break something."

Break something!

"Oh, no," thought Oliver, "Sam's present!"

He quickly took off his knapsack and looked through it. The package seemed to be in one piece.

He sighed and took it out.

"Happy birthday, Sam," he said as he gave her the brightly wrapped package.

"Oh, Oliver, what a surprise! Thank you," she cried.

She carefully unwrapped the present. When she saw what it was, her eyes sparkled.

"Oh, Oliver, Spring Water perfume! You shouldn't have!" she said.

Then she grinned.

"But I'm glad you did," she said.

Sam and Oliver laughed at the same time.

In the meantime students were streaming into school from every direction. Golliwog Day was in full swing. Oliver saw kids carrying dogs, cats, pet canaries, and even snakes! Everyone was laughing and joking as they went into the school building.

"Looks like *everyone* came to school today," said Oliver. "Josh probably won't get a chance to use his attendance program at all."

"Yes," answered Sam. "In fact, I even invited Stinky to stay for the day."

She explained that Rusty had brought Stinky to school with him and asked if he could stay.

"That's right," said Stinky. "I just had to come today. I wouldn't have missed Golliwog Day for the world!"

"By the way," he said to Sam. "If you're the principal, where is the *real* principal and all the teachers?"

"Oh, they're all over in the school office," she answered. "They're going to let the students do everything, but they're standing by just in case...."

"Yes," said Oliver. "The only one really working today is Mr. Huffhauser, the school custodian. He knows where everything is, and he has all the keys for the different rooms."

Just then Jennifer and Kim walked by. They were dressed in matching jeans and had identical sweat shirts that had THE PURPLE WORMS printed on the front.

"Hi!" said Jennifer, waving. "Isn't it a beautiful day?"

Everyone waved back.

"Where are you two going?" asked Sam.

"To the biology room," answered Kim.

"Yes," said Jennifer. "We have a lot of students lined up who want to learn the worm squirm, and it's almost time for class to begin."

Then she looked at her watch.

"Oops! It's already begun!" she cried. "We have to hurry. See you later!"

And with that she and Kim hurried up the stairs and into the school building. Oliver and Sam looked at each other and rolled their eyes.

"I guess I'd better be going too," said Rusty. "I'm a monitor and I'll have to be on duty."

He looked at his cousin and winked.

"Why don't you hang around with Oliver and I'll see you later," he said.

After Rusty left, Oliver went over to his bike. He peeked in on Pom-pom to see if he was all right. But as soon as he did that, Pom-pom started to bark.

"Quiet, Pom-pom," said Oliver as he lifted up the cover of the basket and picked up the little dog. "We'll be on our way in a moment!"

Just then Stinky came over.

"Hey, he's a cute little thing," he said. "Do you mind if I pet him?"

Without waiting for an answer, Stinky took Pom-pom out of Oliver's hands and started to pet him. Suddenly Pom-pom jumped out of his arms.

"Oops!" cried Stinky. "How careless of me."

As soon as Pom-pom was on the ground, he ran over to Irving's cage and barked like crazy. Irving ran around and around his small cage like a dog chasing his own tail. Pom-pom circled the cage and growled and whined and barked, all at the same time.

Oliver ran over to get him, when all of a sudden Irving did something strange. He turned his back to Pom-pom and took a stance.

Everyone watched in fascination as Irving raised his tail.

Oliver was getting a funny feeling about this. He was just about to ask Stinky what was going on, when he saw Irving spray little Pom-pom!

A terrible stink filled the air. It smelled like a thousand rotten eggs had suddenly broken!

Pom-pom yelped as if someone had just stepped on his tail. Then he ran off, crying and yipping.

Oliver heard laughter and turned around just in time to see Stinky crack up.

Then something clattered behind him. He turned again, to see Irving bursting out the door of his cage.

Oliver tried to grab him, but the little skunk was too quick. He ran toward the school steps and the last Oliver saw of him, he was entering the building.

Students ran around all over the place holding their noses and looking wildly around.

"Yuck! What a stink!" someone yelled.

"Let me out of here!" cried someone else.

Dogs barked, cats meowed, and Sam screamed loudest of all.

"De-skunked, huh?" Oliver turned and looked angrily at Stinky, who was giggling with glee.

But Oliver didn't have time to waste—he had

to find Pom-pom, and fast! His mother would never forgive him if anything ever happened to her little dog.

"Quick, Sam," he yelled. "You go after Irving. I'll go after Pom-pom!"

CHAPTER
6

Oliver jumped on his bike, pedaling furiously after Pom-pom. He almost trapped the little dog by the schoolyard fence, but Pompom wiggled under and got away. By the time Oliver rode around, he didn't know which way Pom-pom had gone, but it was easy to figure out. All he had to do was look for people holding their noses and making funny faces. He pumped his pedals faster, following Pom-pom's trail all the way back to Sutherland Avenue.

As Oliver rode he could hear people crying, "Oh, no! It's that kid again!" "Let's get out of here!"

Suddenly, Oliver saw a group of people running and holding their noses.

"Oh, no!" groaned Oliver. The frantic people were running out of—of all places—Webley's Department Store!

"I'd better find Pom-pom before Mr. Quincy does," Oliver told himself.

Oliver jumped off his bike and ran into the store. He was almost knocked over by a man holding a handkerchief over his nose.

"Excuse me, sir, but did anyone see a little dog running around here?" he asked.

"A dog? No. But there is a skunk in the per-*achoo*-fume department." The man gasped. He dashed out of the store as if he'd been chased by a monster.

"That must be Pom-pom!" thought Oliver. He ran toward the same perfume counter where he'd bought Sam's present just a few days before.

Unfortunately, Oliver didn't get far. Just as he was passing the wallets and handbags, he crashed right into Mr. Quincy. He nearly knocked a big cardboard box out of the manager's hands. The box read ONE DOZ. BOTTLES HEAVENLY FRAGRANCE.

But the fragrance coming from the box was anything but heavenly. Mr. Quincy's face was screwed up in a look of distaste as he looked down at Oliver. "You again!" he said.

Right then the top of the box lifted up and Pom-Pom poked his head out.

"Hey! Pom-pom!" cried Oliver happily.

"Of course, this would be *your* dog," said Mr. Quincy. He handed the box to Oliver. But Pom-pom scrambled out and went running between the legs of the shoppers and out the door.

"Come back, Pom-pom! Come back!" shouted Oliver.

"No! Don't come back, Pom-pom! Don't come

back!" Mr. Quincy mopped his face with his handkerchief.

Oliver cut through the crowd of shoppers like a linebacker for his favorite football team. He burst out the door. To his relief, there was Pom-pom, chewing on a pretzel from Nat's Pretzel Cart.

"He's a cute little pooch," Nat told Oliver. "But, boy, could he use a bath!"

Oliver decided there wasn't enough time to explain about the skunk. He'd had enough of Sutherland Avenue for the day—and he guessed Sutherland Avenue had enough of him.

"Poor Pom-pom," he murmured. "You'll be cleaned up in no time. . . . You'd better be, or Mom will kill me!"

When Oliver walked into the vet's office, he saw that the place was packed. It was going to be a long, long wait. "Why did all these animals have to pick Golliwog Day to get sick?" Oliver wondered as he looked around. There were people sitting on sofas and chairs, each one holding a very different pet. The only thing they had in common was the look they gave Oliver and Pom-pom.

"Uh-oh," thought Oliver as he sat down. "I guess they smell Pom-pom. Please, nobody say anything. I'll be soooooo embarrassed!"

The large man in the plaid suit sitting next to Oliver did speak, but it wasn't about Pom-pom. It was about the green parrot he held in the cage on his lap.

"Every morning when Oscar wanted me to put his cage outside in the fresh air, he'd say, 'Oscar's a good boy!' But for the past month Oscar hasn't said a word. I'm worried sick!"

Oliver nodded his head politely. He wished he could think of something to say, but he was too worried about his own pet. Luckily, nobody in the waiting room mentioned poor Pom-pom's smell.

Finally, Oliver relaxed enough to look through some of the pet magazines. He was reading an article called "A Giraffe As a Pet—Is Your Ceiling High Enough?" when the parrot began bobbing his head up and down.

"Oh, look, look!" cried the man in the plaid suit. "Oscar always does that before he speaks. What is it, Oscar? Talk for Daddy!"

By now every head in the place was turned to Oscar. Everyone gasped as the parrot opened his beak to speak.

"*Squuawwwwwk!* What a stink! Get me out of here!"

Oliver could feel himself sinking into the chair.

"Oscar is cured! Oscar is cured! Oh, thank you!" The man sang as he ran out the door, swinging the cage.

"You know something? That parrot was absolutely right," huffed a woman with a Persian cat.

"I was just about to say the same thing!" agreed a man holding a hamster. "It's getting to be too much. I can't stand it!"

"It's that little dog!" shouted a young girl, pointing to Pom-pom.

"You're right," said a boy. "Look at poor Felix here. He doesn't like it at all." He held up his pet snake, who was flicking his tongue out and looking right at Pom-pom.

"I want to go home," cried the little girl.

"She's not the only one," the other people mumbled.

Oliver's cheeks were red as everyone stood up at the same time and rushed out the door.

Just then the doctor's assistant came into the room, calling, "Next?"

Oliver looked around the empty room and shrugged. "I guess that's me." He picked up Pom-pom and walked inside.

After Oliver had explained what had happened, the vet looked at Pom-pom and sighed.

"I'll do the best I can," he said. "But I can't promise that I'll be able to get rid of all the smell. After all, that's a skunk's defense. If the smell were easily gotten rid of, no one would worry about it in the first place."

Oliver thanked the vet and told him to do the best he could. Then he left the office, got on his bike, and headed toward school. He could imagine what was going on there with a wild skunk on the loose!

When he got back to the school, there was no one outside. But inside, he could hear screaming and yelling and barking. "This might be worse than I imagined," he thought as he entered the school building.

The first thing he saw was a big dog chasing an orange tabby cat.

"What's going . . ." he started to say.

Suddenly the cat scooted right between his legs. The dog tried to do the same, but the big animal couldn't fit. It ended up dragging Oliver along on top of it.

"Hey!" yelled Oliver as he held on to the dog's back. "Let me off!"

The dog rounded a corner, and Oliver flew off and crashed to the floor. As he lay there, stunned, three gerbils and a pet squirrel ran over him.

When he finally managed to get up, it was just in time to see another big dog come tearing around the corner, followed by three cats and a raccoon.

The group dashed by him as Oliver flattened himself against the wall. After they passed, Oliver stepped around the corner. Then he saw Mr. Flanders, the English teacher, and Ms. Harmony, the history teacher, come running down the hallway. A gang of students was right behind them.

They were all *running away* from something.

"Hey!" yelled Oliver as the fast-moving bunch zoomed by. "What's going on?"

Ms. Harmony gave him a wild look. Her hair was messed up and her glasses were on crooked. Oliver had never seen her like this. She was usually so calm.

Just as the last of the students ran by, Oliver saw Matthew and Josh, in the rear.

"Matthew, Josh!" Oliver cried. "Hold up! What's the matter with everyone? Has Irving been found?"

"Irving?" cried Josh, skidding to a stop. "Who knows?"

"What do you mean?" asked Oliver.

"Haven't you heard?" answered Matthew, who also stopped. "There are *two* skunks in the school!"

"Two skunks?" said Oliver in amazement.

"That's right," he heard a voice from behind him. He turned and saw Sam running up.

"What two skunks?" replied Oliver. Now he was really confused.

"Those two skunks, Rusty and Stinky," cried Sam angrily. "They exchanged Irving with a skunk named Melvin. And Melvin isn't fixed! It was *Melvin* you took to school today!" Sam glared at Oliver. "I knew you shouldn't have trusted Rusty!"

"But . . ." cried Oliver.

Then he shook his head from side to side and groaned. "Oh, boy! No wonder I heard funny noises coming from around the garage last night. It was Stinky and Rusty exchanging Melvin for Irving!"

"Wait a minute, Oliver," said Sam. "You must have been able to tell that Irving wasn't Irving when you saw him."

"No way," insisted Oliver. "Those skunks must really look alike."

"You'd better believe they do!" answered Sam. "Not only that, but Rusty and Stinky planned the whole thing from the very beginning! They got the idea when I said that I was going to allow pets into school on Golliwog Day."

"But how did Irving get into school?" asked Oliver.

"That little brat Stinky brought him," said Sam. "In fact, it was right after you had left. Stinky went away for a few minutes and came back with Irving in the cage. Then all of a sudden he released Irving!"

"That little stinker!" cried Oliver.

"Yes," agreed Sam. "Then Rusty started to laugh and say that this was going to be the most fun that he had ever had on Golliwog Day."

"But I thought Stinky loved skunks," said Oliver. "Why would he do such a thing?"

"Oh, Stinky loves skunks all right," answered Sam. "But he knows that they won't be harmed. In fact, he had the nerve to say that he wanted his skunks back as soon as possible!"

Oliver lowered his head and groaned again.

"This is all my fault," he said.

"It doesn't matter whose fault it is right now," answered Sam. "The only thing that matters is that we get those two skunks out of the school as soon as possible!"

Oliver asked what was happening at the moment.

"Rusty and Stinky just ran down to the biology room," answered Matthew. "We had reports that one of the skunks was seen there."

"Is that why everyone is running away from there?" asked Oliver.

"Right!" answered Sam. "And that includes Josh and Matthew here. I asked them to help and they just took off!"

Matthew and Josh looked embarrassed.

"We're sorry, Sam," said Matthew. "I guess when we saw the teachers running, we just got panicky."

Sam nodded. "I understand," she said. "But we have to be tough about this. We can't let those skunks run around the school. There'll be a big stink about it later."

"In more ways than one," said Josh.

"This is no time for jokes," cried Oliver. "Come on, let's get to the biology room!"

CHAPTER
7

When they got to the biology room, Oliver saw Jennifer and Kim standing by "Old Bones," a facsimile skeleton that was used for study. The whole science class had put it together last week as a project.

Oliver heard laughter and saw Rusty and Stinky underneath one of the lab tables in the room.

"What are they doing under there?" asked Sam.

"Trying to coax one of the skunks out," answered Jennifer. "They ran in, saying they'd followed one of them in here."

"What happened to your class?" asked Matthew.

"Are you kidding?" said Kim. "As soon as Rusty and Stinky said a skunk was in here, they took off like jack rabbits!"

"I'm just glad I didn't bring Princess Fluffy," Jennifer sniffed. "I'm sure my cat wouldn't like skunks."

Just then Oliver saw a furry black-and-white shape whiz by on the floor.

"There's Irving!" he cried.

Everyone looked to where Oliver had been pointing. And sure enough, there was a skunk running between the lab tables.

"Let's get him!" cried Jennifer.

Rusty and Stinky got out from under one of the tables.

"Be careful with my pet!" yelled Stinky. "I'll sue the school if a hair of his little black-and-white head is harmed!"

Rusty and he burst into another round of laughter and sat down on a lab bench.

"Wait a minute!" yelled Sam. "Suppose that's not Irving, but *Melvin*!"

They all stopped in their tracks as if they were playing statue.

"You're right!" cried Kim.

Jennifer agreed.

"I say we get out of here!" she cried.

Oliver was the first to move again.

"Since this is my fault," he said. "*I'll* stay and capture Irving or Melvin, whichever one he is. Everyone else can go out."

Suddenly the skunk darted right between his legs. Without thinking, Oliver made a grab for it but missed. The little creature ran underneath "Old Bones" and Oliver dove for it. But the skunk ran off and Oliver rammed into the skel-

eton. It wobbled on its stand for a moment and then started to fall over.

"Look out!" he heard someone yell.

The next thing Oliver knew, there was a crash, and "Old Bones" fell to the floor. As soon as it did, it broke into pieces.

There were bones everywhere!

Just as Oliver stood up from the floor holding a tibia in his hand, a Great Dane and a French poodle trotted past the door. They spotted what was left of "Old Bones" on the floor and did a quick double-take. Licking their chops, they made a beeline for the biology room and the tempting pile of treats.

Jennifer flapped her arms and ran to stop them, but the dogs grabbed the bones and ran off.

"Oh, great!" she cried. "Those dogs are running off with 'Old Bones'!"

Kim shook her head. "Oliver, the class worked so hard on that project. They'll never forgive you," she warned.

Oliver felt like crawling into a hole somewhere. He didn't know what to say, so he kept on looking around for Irving instead.

"There he goes!" cried Matthew, who was pointing to a bushy tail disappearing out the open door.

"Who left the door open, as if I didn't know?" said Sam with an angry look at Rusty and Stinky.

"Gosh," said Rusty innocently. "Can't you people catch two little skunks?"

"Yeah," added Stinky. "It seems like those

two skunks are making *monkeys* out of all of you!"

Then without another word they ran out into the hall.

Oliver sat down on a bench. He was still holding one bone in his hand. He looked at it, wondering how it got there.

The rest of the gang stood by quietly.

Suddenly Sam cried, "Hey, let's not fall apart like 'Old Bones.' It's not the end of the world!"

"It might as well be," said Oliver with a groan.

"Don't be silly," answered Sam. "If we stick together, we can figure out what to do next."

"Speaking of that," said Josh, "what *do* we do next?"

As if in answer to his question, Mr. Huffhauser, the school custodian, burst into the room.

"Which one of you kids is Oliver?" he cried.

"I am," answered Oliver.

"Well, one of your skunks is trapped in the school auditorium," said Mr. Huffhauser. "So if you want to get him, you'd better come!"

Everyone jumped up at the same time. Oliver and Sam took the lead and headed for the auditorium.

When they got there, it sounded and looked like a zoo. There were animals running all over the place. There were even a few parakeets flying around.

Kids were trying to keep their pets quiet, but it was no use. Barks, meows, screams, and yells echoed off the walls.

"Oliver!" yelled a voice. Oliver looked over to

see Mr. Thompson, the school principal. Usually, he was the neatest person in the school. Today his jacket was off, his tie was pulled to one side, and the tails of his shirt stuck out of his pants.

"You've got to get your skunk out of here immediately before the animals go completely crazy!" Mr. Thompson begged.

Oliver gulped. "Wh-where is he?" he asked.

Mr. Thompson pointed to the stage. Oliver and Sam both looked. There was Irving, climbing up the curtains!

"Quick, Sam," yelled Oliver. "Help me get him!"

Oliver ran to the stage and jumped up onto it. Sam was right behind him. Irving was trying to climb up to get away from the dogs and cats that were scurrying around all over the place.

Oliver had just reached Irving, when all of a sudden he raised his tail.

"Oh, no!" cried Sam. "I don't think that's Irving. It must be Melvin!"

"What'll I do!" yelled Oliver.

"Quick, grab his two hind legs and squeeze them together!" answered Sam.

"What good will that do?" asked Oliver as he did it anyway.

"I heard somewhere that you can keep a skunk from spraying that way," yelled Sam.

"Well, you know it and I know it," yelled Oliver back. "But do skunks know it?"

Oliver now held the skunk backwards, its

black-and-white head sticking out from under his arm. He held the skunk's two hind legs firmly together.

"What happens now?" said Oliver. "If I let go, he's going to spray me."

"Wait a minute," continued Sam. "You told me once that you can calm down an angry cat by putting a blanket over it. Maybe the same thing works for skunks. Hold on to him while I get something."

"Do I have a choice?" asked Oliver.

Sam grabbed a school pennant off the wall.

"Here!" she cried as she covered the skunk with it. "Now let's get him out of here!"

Oliver ran out of the auditorium with the covered skunk and Sam followed him.

"Where's his cage?" asked Oliver.

"I left it in the school office," said Sam. "Follow me!"

When they got to the office, it was filled with teachers. They all had dazed looks on their faces. Some were sitting and panting.

"Look out, live skunk!" yelled Oliver as he burst into the office, the skunk beneath the pennant.

The office emptied in seconds. Even the teachers who had been panting got up with a burst of new energy.

Oliver went to a corner and sat down in a chair.

He was still holding the skunk's legs as he murmured, "Easy there. You're safe now. Just take it easy."

A few moments went by and Oliver could feel the little animal start to relax. When it finally stopped squirming, he told Sam to lift off the pennant. The little skunk seemed to have calmed down.

"Get the cage, Sam," he said.

Sam got the cage, and ever so gently Oliver released the skunk's legs and put him in. The skunk shuffled over to a corner and lay down.

"Whew!" sighed Oliver. "That was close. Now all we have to do is get one more skunk and we've got this thing licked."

"I certainly hope so," said Sam. "Boy, what a Golliwog Day this turned out to be!"

CHAPTER
8

"**I**'ll take Melvin outside," said Oliver. "We don't want to take a chance of his escaping again."

Sam said that in the meantime she would see what was going on in the rest of the school.

Oliver went into the hall and saw Rusty and Stinky down at the other end.

"Hey!" yelled Oliver.

Rusty and Stinky turned to look in his direction.

Oliver held up the cage.

"I've got Melvin!" he called. "I'm taking him outside."

"Well, that's real good," yelled Rusty.

But by the way he said it, Oliver knew he wasn't sincere. "Boy," he thought, "when this is over, I'm going to give Rusty and Stinky a piece of my mind."

"Yeah," agreed Stinky. "You did very well, Oliver."

Then he held up a paper bag.

"Irving will be easy to capture," he said. "I've got some skunk treats in here. All we have to do is show them to him and he'll come running."

Oliver said that he hoped so. Then he turned and went out of the school building. He walked slowly to his bike, and when he got there, he laid the cage on the ground and sat down. He stared straight ahead.

"It's just not fair," he thought. "Rusty and Stinky tricked me from the very beginning." Now everybody was probably blaming him for everything. Not only that, but it was his fault, too, that Pom-pom got sprayed. His mother's little dog was probably going to stink for weeks. He could just imagine what Mom was going to say about *that*.

He was still feeling gloomy when he saw Sam coming over to him.

"Well, we finally got all the pets quieted down and back to their owners," she said. "Now, if we can only capture Irving, we can get back to normal."

"I guess you think it's all my fault," said Oliver miserably.

Sam smiled.

"I guess I did kind of blame you at the beginning," she admitted. "But when I saw how Rusty and Stinky had tricked you, and how mean they were being, I couldn't stay mad."

Oliver brightened up.

"That's great, Sam," he said.

Just then they saw Rusty and Stinky come out of the building and go over to a low window.

"What's going on?" called Sam.

"We know that Irving is in this room," Rusty yelled back. "But he's hiding on us."

"Yeah, he loves to play hide-and-seek," said Stinky. "But we're going to trick him."

Oliver saw that they were putting the skunk treats on the windowsill. They looked like little dog biscuits to him.

Rusty and Stinky bent down low and hid beneath the window. Suddenly Oliver saw a furry black-and-white figure hop on top of the windowsill.

It was Irving!

Irving started to eat the skunk treats. Then Rusty and Stinky jumped up at the same time and made a grab for him.

But Irving did something very strange. He turned his back, stood up on his front legs, and raised his tail!

"Hey, wait!" yelled Rusty.

But before Rusty could say another word, Irving sprayed him and Stinky!

"*Aaarrgh!*" screamed Rusty.

"*Yeeoow!*" screamed Stinky.

Sam and Oliver could smell the foul odor from where they were. They looked at each other in amazement.

"What's going on?" asked Sam. "I thought Irving was fixed."

"Irving is fixed." Oliver grinned.

"So how could he spray anyone?" asked Sam.

"The answer is very simple," answered Oliver with delight. "It's because that's not Irving on the windowsill. That's Melvin. This is Irving."

And with that, he peeked into the cage.

"Irving, you little devil you. You never said a word about it!"

Sam looked at Oliver for a moment and then burst out laughing. In the meantime, Stinky and Rusty were tearing off their jackets and yelling at the top of their lungs.

A crowd of students came out of the school to see what was going on. When they got a whiff of Rusty and Stinky, they ran off in every direction.

Jennifer, Kim, Josh, and Matthew were among the students who had piled out of the school building. When they saw Oliver and Sam, they came over.

"Hey, what's happening?" asked Jennifer.

"Oh, nothing much," answered Oliver, still trying to hold in the giggles. "Stinky is just living up to his name!"

When Sam heard that, she burst into another fit of laughter. The rest of the gang looked on in confusion, until Oliver told them what had happened.

"Good for them," said Kim. "They deserve

it. They ruined Golliwog Day for the whole school!"

Sam looked at her watch.

"Wait a minute," she said. "It's only twelve o'clock. We have the whole afternoon yet. I'm going to make this Golliwog Day the best one ever—even though it stinks."

The gang looked at her again and then they got the joke.

"That joke smells!" yelled Oliver. "But you're right. We shouldn't let those two human skunks ruin the whole day for us."

"But Melvin is still loose," said Josh. "We can't do anything until he's captured."

"I've got an idea," said Oliver.

He took the cage with Irving in it and walked up to the windowsill, where Melvin was busy eating the skunk treats.

"Oliver, are you crazy?" yelled Sam. "You'll get sprayed!"

"Shhh!" said Oliver. "Everybody stay calm and don't move. Melvin won't spray me unless he thinks he's in danger."

Oliver walked up to the windowsill and placed the cage with Irving right on it. Melvin went up and sniffed. Then he started to scratch at the door, trying to get in. Oliver carefully opened the door and Melvin walked quietly in.

Oliver picked up the cage and went over to where Rusty and Stinky were sitting down on a bench, looking miserable.

"I believe these two skunks belong to you

two skunks," said Oliver, barely controlling his laughter.

He laid the cage down next to them and quickly walked away. The stink was just too much! When he got back to the rest of the kids, he said, "I don't think they'll be able to handle two skunks on their bikes. And no bus driver in his right mind is going to let those two on his bus. I think Rusty and Stinky are going to have to walk home today."

"Yeah, and take tomato juice baths!" laughed Sam.

Then she turned to everyone and said, "We're wasting time talking about those two zeros. Let's get back to school and enjoy the rest of the day."

At the end of the day Sam accompanied Oliver to the vet's to pick up Pom-pom.

"Boy, what a great Golliwog Day it turned out to be," said Sam.

Oliver nodded.

"Yes, we did have a great time," he agreed. "In spite of Rusty and Stinky."

"It's a good thing that Melvin sprayed only those two and not anyone else in the school," said Sam. "Otherwise we might not have school for weeks, until they got rid of the smell."

When Sam said that, it reminded Oliver of Pom-pom.

"Oh, no!" he groaned. "Pom-pom got sprayed! How are we going to get rid of his smell?"

"Let's see how he is first," answered Sam.

*　　*　　*

When they arrived at the vet's Pom-pom was waiting for them. He smelled pretty good from a distance, but when they got real close, there was still a strong whiff of skunk on him.

"The smell should go away completely in a day or two," explained the vet. "In the meantime, I guess you're going to have to bear it."

Oliver picked up Pom-pom and thanked the vet. Then he and Sam went outside.

"I wish there were some way I could make Pom-pom smell better," he said. "I can't bring him home this way."

Suddenly Sam snapped her fingers.

"I've got it!" she cried.

She took out her bottle of Spring Water perfume and shook some drops on Pom-pom. Then she rubbed the perfume into his fur. They both got close to Pom-pom and sniffed.

"How's that?" asked Sam.

"Well, now he smells like Spring Water." Oliver grinned. "But I guess that beats smelling like Skunk!"

Sam laughed as she got on her bike.

"Come on, Oliver," she said. "Let's go home. I'm hungry, and the only thing I want to smell now is supper!"

Oliver went to his bicycle, then stopped. "Sam?" he asked. "Can we please take another route home today?"

Sam shrugged. "Okay with me," she said. "Which way would you like to go?"

"Anywhere but Sutherland Avenue!" Oliver rolled his eyes and put Pom-pom into his bike basket.

Then, with a laugh, the two friends began to slowly bike their way home.